THE SKYJUMPER

THE HIDDEN UPSIDE-DOWN FORCE

By

Glenda Walker

THE SKYJUMPER
THE HIDDEN UPSIDE-DOWN FORCE
by Glenda Walker

Glenda Walker The Skyjumper: The Hidden Upside-Down Force

ISBN 978-1-09834-129-9

Printed in the United States of America First Edition 2021

www.theskyjumper.com

trytheskyjumper@gmail.com

Cover design by Landon Wilson

The Skyjumper
P.O. Box 1051 Dept. SKYJUMPER
Groton, CT. 06340

To my editors Laura and Diana.
It all began in the cockpit.

To Professor Fran Moulder and Desiree for
believing in my writing and that the sky is the limit.

To my husband, Howard, who would go
to the ends of the earth with me.

And to my friends and family. You
are my shooting stars.

−Glenda

CHAPTER ONE

Bzzt. The lights flickered out.

"Are you kidding me?" Dad shouted from his office at the bottom of the stairs. "Boys! Did one of you turn off the lights again?"

Zack darted into our room, hurdling video game cases and collectible action figures. I shook my head as he flung himself through the dimly lit room onto his bed. I knew by the grin on his face that he'd been up to his old tricks.

"Must be the power!" Zack called down. This was actually a believable story. Our home was a creaky, pumpkin blue, rustic farmhouse, surrounded by overgrown bushes. It was built on an island in the Pacific Ocean so isolated that only boats connected us to other towns. Wind often whipped at the island, so a power outage did not seem out of place. It was no surprise that power outages had been plaguing Tarrytown for the last three years, and the past two months had been the toughest. Even the backup generators had started malfunctioning. Our dad had been working around the clock to find the cause.

"Did you turn off the lights again, bro?" I asked. "You know he is seriously going to lose it one of these days."

Zack shrugged. "Not the lights exactly." Lately, it seemed like my brother had to turn everything into a game. But we were twins. We looked alike, sounded the same, and did pretty much everything together. That meant that when Zack caused trouble, I got wrapped up in the stakes.

"Wait… the power box? I can't believe you!" I shouted. "You c-c-could have blown a fuse or something. You know we're both going to get heat for this."

I shoved my book aside on my desk. I rolled up a ketchup stained t-shirt from the floor and threw it at him. My aim was off, though. It landed in the middle of the floor like a deflated parachute.

"Relax, bro," said Zack. "I know how circuits work. I just need to turn the switches back on in the panel box. For now, think of it as Zack's Blackout!"

Zack had a point. Video games weren't the only place where his problem-solving skills shined. Out of the two of us, Zack was the coolest science geek I'd ever known.

Suddenly, the spicy smell of Mom's homemade tomato sauce wafted up the vents and up my nose. My stomach made a low growl. "You know Mom is making lasagna, and you just made the oven go off. She is going to flip!"

As Dad always said, Mom may have been five foot nothing, with wavy, dark brown hair and an innocent brown freckled face, but her voice could break the sound barrier when she wanted to be heard.

We listened to the faint sounds of switch flicking and grumbling from downstairs until at last the lights buzzed back to life.

I can see why a lot of kids at school pointed fingers at Zack for the town-wide blackouts. The first ever blackout happened the first day of school. It was caused by a student. None other than you-know-who. And a week later, Zack rigged the lights to go off during his English test.

For that, he served time in Tarry Middle School Detention Room. And of course, Mom banned him from playing video games. But the kids blaming Zack were wrong now. These days, his pranks were just aimed at our dad.

Zack's campaign to get Dad to pay more attention to us had been going on for two months now, about as long as the increased power outages. The real ones, I mean. Before Zack's Blackouts, he had hidden Dad's favorite reading glasses, prank called his office phone, repeatedly rang the back porch doorbell, and once even released a toad in his office. Anything to pull him away from his work. I understood where he was coming from.

Just then, Mom's voice echoed up the stairs. "Zack and Mack, you are in deep trouble!"

I'm not sure if it was because of the malfunctioning cooling unit or Mom's you're-in-for-it voice, but I could feel sweat beading on my forehead. Not Zack, though. He just grinned at me over the math book we were supposed to be studying. A jagged Jack O' Lantern had nothing on his smile. We sprawled on our beds, pretending to do homework.

Mom's footsteps creaked up the staircase and down the hall. She rushed in our doorway, where she flashed one of her glares that I swear could sear a hole in a wall.

"You know, Dad's not in his office playing video games," she hollered. "He's actually working on something really important, and he needs to concentrate. You may think that turning off the power is funny, but all you're doing is making things difficult. He could have lost some important work, you know."

Zack bit his lip and awkwardly thumbed at his math book. For once, he wasn't wearing his usual half-smirk.

Mom's look softened as she finally realized what I'd known all along. She sighed. "I know you miss him, honey."

"It's no big deal," groaned Zack. "I was just messing around. I'll stop. I know his work's important."

"Not as important as you two," Mom said. She sat on the edge of his bed and ruffled his hair.

Zack jerked away. "Mom, stop!"

"Oh, all right!" she said. "Tell you what. The sooner Dad can finish his work, the sooner things can get back to normal. And boys, let me be clear with you. If you pull another stunt like that, then it's no video games for a month. But if you can get through one week with no pranks, and you both get all your homework done,

I'll call a family no-work day. We can do whatever you want. Deal?"

"Okay. Deal," Zack said. I nodded in agreement.

"Try not to b-b-blow it, Zack," I said as Mom headed back downstairs to the kitchen. It was Monday night, so we just had to make it to the next Monday with no stunts. "Remember that when you get in trouble, we both pay. Come on, let's get our homework done so we can get gaming. And Dad can get his work done too. The Video Game King will be back in no time, just like old times."

Zack sighed. "If he doesn't grow into his office chair first."

CHAPTER TWO

Our dad used to tell nerdy jokes and school us on how to build blanket forts. He was our video game hero, and Zack and I both missed hanging out with him. Still, it seemed to hit Zack harder.

The new Dad, well, his brain seemed to be on a different circuit. He worked for a satellite company headquartered in Washington D.C., and he knew everything there was to know about space exploration. You'd think he would have worked at NASA, but he preferred the cozy cockpit of his home office, where he'd spent all his time since the outages started.

It was Thursday night, and Zack and I were in the kitchen slurping root beer floats when Dad finally emerged from the cockpit. So far, Zack had managed to go three whole days without distracting him from work.

"Boys," he nodded, shuffling down the hall in a computer daze. Like most nights, he joined Mom in the living room with his dinner, and we heard the TV switch on.

"And Mom says I spend too much time looking at screens," Zack mumbled into his glass.

"Is he getting a dad gut?" I whispered. "Looks like his buttons are about to blow off his shirt. And it isn't from Mom's awesome cooking." I heard Mom tell him that he needed to take walks or start working out. But I noticed by the end of the day, Dad was mentally exhausted. Since the blackouts began, Mom and Dad ended up falling asleep on the overstuffed vintage sofas. We had inherited our old furniture from our dad's parents along with the house. The old, overstuffed sofas were only comfortable for so long, so our parents regularly woke up at 2 am, when ancient comedy shows were on.

Without them noticing, Zack had reprogrammed the volume level on the remote control, so we'd definitely hear those theme songs from our room and knew we would have plenty of warning when they turned off the TV. Better yet, they tripped their way upstairs to look in on us before going to bed themselves. We could easily turn off our games and jump back into bed and slip under our blankets, pretending to sleep.

This was the life our parents seemed to be content with living in "Teary Town," as Zack cleverly named it. It was the same work routine, the same conversations, the same TV shows. They didn't socialize much, and I couldn't remember the last time we took a family trip or did something just for the fun of it.

Tarrytown, as it was really called, seemed like a perfect name for our outdated coastal suburbia. We passed our days there waiting for the town to build an entertainment center, but they never did. The entire population of twelve hundred and seven was boring except for me, Zack, and our friends. Everyone else walked around on autopilot. If things were going to change, it was up to us to make it happen.

I think that's why Zack had started stirring things up a bit. We didn't want to live everyday like those late-night reruns on TV. We wanted excitement. We needed action!

"And...action!" Zack said, jostling my shoulders later that night. "They're asleep."

I opened one eye and squinted at the glowing numbers on our clock a few feet in front of my bed. It was 12:07 a.m.

"You sure?" I mumbled, remembering that we were already one strike from a video game ban.

"Yep! Just checked the living room," Zack said with a sly grin. "Like clockwork. Time for some serious game playing."

Zack and I were identical in a lot of ways, from the dark, curly hair and deep-set blue eyes we got from Mom to the oval-shaped red freckled faces we inherited from Dad. But our attitude toward video games was the biggest difference between us. Yes, I liked games too, but I wasn't a serious gamer like he was. What I really wanted was more action in the real world. The one where you didn't just wake up and wonder what the new day would bring, but where something actually happened. For Zack, though, video games were a perfect escape from a world that wasn't quite enough for him, especially living in Tarrytown.

"I call RoboTron!" said Zack, switching on the futuristic mission to Mars and selecting the only camouflage metal-armored character. Video games were also a chance for us to take a break from being identical, so we always created two characters that looked totally different.

On top of that, our rhyming names always caused loads of problems both at home and at school.

So as Zack keyed in ZackAttack as his player's name, he added, "And you'd better not use MackAttack. What were Mom and Dad thinking when they gave us weird rhyming names?"

"Don't you remember? Mom says we were named after Uncle Zackery Mack, her astronaut big brother," I said. "But you know, I'm getting tired of being called 'Zack or Mack' in one breath as if we aren't two different people. It sounds like someone's ordering a drive-thru fast food meal."

"At least Sol stopped calling us both 'Ack!' Do you remember that? I told him that if I beat him at MegaRacer, he'd have to quit," said Zack. I thought back to when Sol used to hang out with us, usually working his way to the middle of the room to commandeer the chip bowl. The rest of us, a head taller and more focused on gaming, would aim our controllers right over his bushy, blonde afro. Zack shrugged. "Easy fix."

"Oh yes," I laughed "Still, it would be nice if people could actually tell us apart."

"Yeah, they should all know by now that I'm the slightly more handsome one," Zack said.

"Nice try, bro, but I don't see any girls crushing on you," I said, reaching my arms out from the bottom of the bed and shoving him aside.

"The only crushing you need to be thinking about right now is crushing this game," said Zack. He gripped the controller tight as he honed in on the space race.

"Hey Zack, move over. I'm ready," I said and climbed out of bed to sit beside him. Even if being identical had a few downsides, it was neat always having my brother by my side. And now, we had a long night of gaming ahead of us. No need to worry about the time. We didn't even mind that we had school in the morning. If we heard the canned laughter from the TV downstairs, we'd be safe.

CHAPTER THREE

The next morning, the alarm clock beeped from our dresser across the room. Zack sprang out of bed to turn it off.

"No snoozing for us." I groaned. "How do you have so much energy after so little sleep?"

"Come on, bro," he said. "If Mom sees how tired you are, she might suspect that we stayed up late. Besides, we have to catch the bus."

In a flurry, Zack and I threw on wrinkled navy polo shirts and khaki shorts, ran down to the kitchen, and scarfed down some waffles. We quickly grabbed our backpacks and raced down our driveway. From there, I dragged myself over one street to Tarry Highway to wait at our bus stop.

While Zack usually slept during the ride, I smiled as I settled in my seat to watch "rush hour." In Tarrytown, that meant about seven cars and a few cargo trucks on the road. I listened intently to a foghorn fading in the distance. After driving through the town business center, we passed the only active church up on the hill. Zack would always wake up to the sound of the lone clock tower ringing at exactly 7 a.m. Lately, the time had been more sporadic because of the blackouts. Zack would peep out the window at the white cross towering behind the church steeple, shining like a beacon as it reflected the morning sun. And every time, he'd shake his head and drift back to sleep.

After an hour ride, there it was, set in the lone back woods. Tarrytown Middle School, no points for imagination on the name, was a long, cracked red brick building filled with old desks and lockers that needed their hinges oiled. School life was pretty much like life in general in 'Teary Town.' Each day was like the one before it.

Zack and I didn't see each other much in class, since he was in Algebra 2 and all advanced subjects except English. Zack was fortunate, he'd inherited our parents' math genes. Mom was a math teacher. She'd been named teacher of the year for starting a young math ambassadors' program. That's how Mom met Dad. She took her students to a space exploration conference where, according to Dad, she fell in love by the end of the keynote speech. Somehow those math genes skipped me, though. I was in Honors English and not so great in Pre-Algebra. Back in sixth grade, Zack and I had tried taking each other's midterm tests. Zack had gotten me a perfect math score plus a ten-point bonus, and I got him an A- on his English Quiz. We wound up serving a couple of days of detention because the teachers thought our scores were suspicious. I don't know what Zack was thinking. Never in a million years could I have earned an A on any math test, not to mention bonus points. Mom had grounded us from video games for a week after the principal called her about it. So now, we stayed out of each other's classes. We always sat together at lunch, though.

Today was Pizza Friday, so we walked into the rubbery cheese smell and echoing shouts of the school cafeteria. Scanning the rectangular tables in the back corner where the eighth graders clumped, we spotted our best friend, Jordan. He was tan skinned with a shock of curly brown hair raised up on his head like a fancy top hat. At the moment, he was bent over a bagel, spreading jelly and cream cheese, and we climbed into the empty seats next to him.

"Hey guys," said Jordan. "You have got to come over this weekend and see this new game I've got. It's unlike anything I've ever played before."

"New game?" asked Zack, pushing his tray of mashed potatoes aside to give his full attention to the subject. "What's it called?"

"It's called," Jordan paused to sip his chocolate milk for dramatic effect, "The Skyjumper."

"Cool!" said Zack. "I haven't heard of that one. I usually know about every new game that gets released."

Jordan said, "Well, it's going to be the next big thing. Trust me."

"Where'd you get it?" Zack continued. "Have you started it yet?"

"Is it multi-player?" I chimed in.

Without notice, Jordan jumped up. "I almost forgot, I've got to run. Orthodontist appointment. But come over as soon as you can so I can show you. You're going to love this game, I promise." Jordan flashed his braces, then grabbed his lunch and dashed out.

"That was kind of weird," said Zack.

"Nah, I mean, no, he always goes to the ortho during lunch," I said. "That way he can skip Study Hall in the afternoon."

"Oh, right," said Zack. "Anyway, can you believe it? A new game that even *I've* never heard of! The Skyjumper. Do you think it's jet fighting? An intergalactic mission?"

"Sounds interesting, bro," I said, "but unlike you, I need to study for this math test."

As I pulled out my math book to prepare for my test, I saw Zack look at the table beside us, the one where Amanda and Sol were laughing. Zack used to be friends with them before Amanda beat him at NBA Hoops Challenge and he declared her his arch-nemesis for life.

Now, as he sat at the table with his dentist-going friend's bagel crumbs and his studious brother, I wondered if he regretted that decision.

I got my answer soon enough. He picked up his straw and blew the wrapper directly into Amanda's pile of fries. Even though she hadn't seen him do it, she looked right at Zack. "You missed," she said, throwing the wrapper in the trash. "Guess you still need work on your aim, ZackAttack."

"Nah," he said. "That went right where I was aiming."

As the bell rang, I looked at my brother. "You have got to s-s-start finding some better ways to get people's attention."

CHAPTER 4

"What?!" Zack cried. "I was just about to beat you! The power always cuts out when I'm about to get to the next level."

It was Saturday night, and we were almost to the end of one of my favorite video games, Stronghold Master Warrior 2. We'd battled forces for three hours straight while our parents slept in front of the TV. When the power cut out, our game suddenly ended, and we were in the dark.

"Just another blackout," I said. I smiled and added, "I guess now we'll never know who won."

"One thing we do know," said Zack, "is that I had nothing to do with the town's blackouts. Everyone in this town knows I wouldn't cut the power during a video game."

"I'll vouch for you. You were home gaming." I said. Zack had been getting a lot of blame for outages he didn't cause. Sure, he brought it on himself with all the other pranks he pulled at school. But even though it was too dark to see his face, twins know things, and I could tell that all of this blame was getting to him. "I'll help you make sure they finally believe that ZackAttack is not cutting the town's power as a prank. I knew all along you weren't doing it. Sorry people were spreading rumors."

I stood up and stared out the window. The few houses nearby were blacked out, too. It wasn't just our house. It was a moonless night, and it was so dark it was like looking into a bottomless pit.

"It's probably not going to come back on for a while," I said. "I guess we might as well go to bed."

"Hey," said Zack, "maybe we could get up early and go to Jordan's to play that Skyjumper game."

"He's got church in the morning," I said.

"Oh, right," said Zack. "What do you think about that religious stuff?"

"You mean church?" I said. "I guess I haven't thought about it much." Well, now that you'd asked, living in a place like "Teary Town" where nothing really happened gave me a lot of time to wonder about the point of it all. Zack had never wanted to move to Tarrytown from Washington D.C. in the first place. I'd always thought that Zack's goofing off was because, living in this boring town and adapting to Dad's hectic work schedule, he was just looking for something to do. But maybe he was looking for something bigger.

"What about you?" I asked him. "What do you believe in?"

Silence filled the darkness for a moment. Then, I heard Zack fling his blanket across the room and knock over his collection of video game action figures. It was another muggy night. The air conditioner unit wasn't working. "Going to church isn't going to fix the outages, and it's not going to bring our family back together."

But then he added, "Maybe we already have the knowledge we need to fix our own problems, and we just need to figure out how to use it."

CHAPTER FIVE

"These outages have gotten ridiculous!" Dad shouted. It was Sunday evening, and the power had finally come back on. Dad was cutting a jagged piece of steak as if it were an ancient animal tissue in a science experiment. "The electric company doesn't do a thing about it. How much longer do they expect us to wait for them to tear out the old system and replace it? Just because we live in Tarrytown…"

Zack mumbled, "You mean *Teary.*"

Dad continued, "…it doesn't mean we can wait forever. How can we get anything done when the power's so unreliable?"

"You're right, David," Mom said. "I've got to grade my students' math tests. I've called and left messages on a recording, and the town council has called Tarrytown

Utilities so many times to complain, but nobody seems to pay attention to us."

"It's not right," he muttered, poking at a piece of steak and stuffing it into his mouth. "They can't continue to ignore us and focus only on larger cities. We pay our taxes, too. Just goes to show, if you want something done around here, you've got to do it yourself--"

"So," Mom interrupted, digging into her baked potato as she cut him off. She glanced at me and Zack, looking determined to change the subject. "How is your homework coming along?"

Suddenly, the lights flickered like Morse Code. They flared so brightly I thought the bulbs were going to blow, then they dimmed and went out.

"Not again!" Dad cried, tossing his fork and knife onto the plate. "This is ridiculous! How are we supposed to…?"

"I'll call the mayor's office in the morning," Mom said, laying a hand on Dad's shoulder. "You're right. We should get a credit on our bill at the very least."

With that, Dad helped her gather battery-powered candles and flashlights. "I appreciate your help, Audrie."

The power was out for a few hours, and by the time it came back on, Zack was bouncing like a tennis ball from room to room from boredom while our parents snoozed on the couch. He knew that he just had one day left that he needed to keep out of trouble. I wasn't sure he could avoid getting games taken away and earn some time with Dad. But with his homework finished and the power out, it took everything in him not to stir things up. The moment the lights flickered back on, Zack raced upstairs to continue his game. I finished my chapter in "Off the Grid" before trudging up after him. My brother had a seriously one-track mind.

The following day, a cloudy Monday morning, we weren't so fortunate. We were at school when the power phased in and out for a few hours. Our teachers had started keeping flashlights and lanterns handy. Students turned them on and placed them around the classroom while the teachers continued their lessons.

After school, Jordan caught up with us. "Hey, you guys. How come you didn't come over this weekend?"

"Sorry," I said. "We got busy with chores. When the power was on, that is."

Jordan said, "Well, you should come to my house after dinner tonight. The Skyjumper awaits."

"Definitely!" Zack shouted.

"Umm. Wait a second. If the power's out, how are we going to play?"

"Don't worry about it," Jordan said. "The Skyjumper is different than other games. It holds enough charge to last for days, so we can play it whether the power's on or not. And that's just one of the many awesome things about it. Catch you later!"

Later, after we came home from school, Zack found Mom in the kitchen. "You know it's Monday, Mom?" he said.

"I suppose it is," she said. "Is there something important about that?"

Zack shrugged. "Well, I've done all my homework and stayed out of Dad's way, and you said that we could have a family no-work day to play video games togeth-"

Just then, the power went out completely.

"Oh, not again!" Mom said. "I'm sorry honey, but your dad and I will need to deal with the power outage. Besides, we can't play video games without electricity. It will have to wait."

At dinner, Dad said, "This happened last month, one county over from us. One of my research colleagues mentioned it, and their power was out for a full week! Because our population's so small, it's not a power company's priority to get to us quickly. It would take them at least that long to fix our generator and maybe even longer."

"A week!" I exclaimed. "Or longer?" I couldn't believe what I was hearing.

Zack just sat there with his mouth hanging open as if he had a kickstand parked in his mouth.

"I'll never survive without video games for an entire week," Zack finally said once he got his voice back. I knew he was thinking about family no-work day, too.

All I could think about was how much complaining Dad was going to do.

Mom laughed. "That's all you worry about, Zack? Why don't you play outside, ride your bike, you know, all those things kids used to do before there were video games. Or if you're really bored, I've noticed your room could use a good cleaning."

After dinner, Zack had a better idea. He couldn't take living in the darkness any longer. He invited me to join him, but that was out of the question. I had to finish my science homework.

"Hey, Mom, you got a spare flashlight?" Zack asked. "I want to ride over to Jordan's house to do some homework."

Mom sighed. "How many times have I told you to replace the light on your bike?"

"I promise I'll do it," Zack said softly. "But we've got a big test this week and I know Jordan can help me ace it." Now, Zack was flailing his hands in front of his face, his voice rising in pitch.

I could barely wipe the smirk from my face. Tonight, his performance was worthy of an Oscar.

"Okay," Mom said. "Don't forget your phone. Call me when you get to Jordan's house!"

"But Jordan only lives a few streets away," Zack replied.

"I don't care. I want to know you're safe," she said.

For a second, I was nervous for Zack to go by himself. It was pitch black out there. But he took the flashlight from her hand and walked out into the unsavory black hole of our front yard. As soon as he got to his bike, though, a smile crossed his face.

"Skyjumper, meet your match!"

CHAPTER SIX

Zack taped the flashlight to the middle of the rusted handlebars of his bike. The original light had long since broken, but he'd never bothered to replace it. Though the scuffed, once black mountain bike looked like it had survived a drop in the Grand Canyon, there was no question of replacing it. Zack set his timer on his phone and stuffed it into his back pocket. He settled onto the peeling seat and zoomed off into the night.

Following the shaky flashlight beam, he skillfully navigated the dark street. He'd been riding this route since the fifth grade, so he had it memorized. He grinned.

"Can't wait to play the newest, hottest video game on the entire planet." He popped a wheelie. "Skyjumper! I can't wait!" he hollered, his voice echoing in the dark.

He rode two blocks before seeing even one car on Farm Street. Even though the farmhouse style homes on this street were more modern, they spread out on large lots, so even when the lights were on, the street was still fairly dark. It seemed like the entire neighborhood was hibernating.

He turned a corner onto Bank Street to reach Jordan's house. Framed by a pathway of trees, a circular driveway flanked a huge porch. Sometimes on hot summer nights, he and Jordan sat on the swing and played handheld games.

Zack's timer ended with a roar. He arrived at the house in record time, two minutes flat, beating his own record by sixteen

seconds. Zack seesawed his legs off the bike and propped it against the bottom of the three cement steps.

The flashlight was dangling off the handlebar, the gray duct tape starting to unravel. He considered switching it off but figured he didn't want to leave his bike in complete darkness. Stepping up to the porch, he was about to knock on the door when Jordan's mom surprised him by opening it. She must have heard his footsteps.

"Oh, hello, Zack," she said, standing in a yellow pool of lantern light. "You just missed Jordan. He left me a note to tell you that he rode over to Sol's house to do some homework. Maybe you can catch him."

Why would he leave a note instead of just texting me? Zack wondered. *And since when does he do homework with Sol?*

Zack shrugged it off and leapt off the porch. He turned to ask Jordan's mom about the new video game, but she was already shutting the door. *Not a good idea anyway,* he thought. *Maybe Jordan hasn't told her about it yet.*

He pulled out his phone and speed-dialed home. Mom picked up on the first ring.

"You get there okay?" she asked.

"Yeah, but Jordan went to Sol's house to do homework, so I'll ride over there." Zack thought maybe he should call him.

Mom repeated, "Be careful, Zack."

"Huh? Oh, yeah. Okay, Mom."

Zack heard the door behind him finally click shut when he jumped on his bike and started pedaling. Steering his bike with his phone and hand gripped to the handlebar, he headed toward Sol's house on Minor

Street in the opposite direction. The street became more of a lane, as there were few houses that way. Open fields oozing liquid darkness morphed into dense woods. He rode hard into a pothole, skidded, and fell forward off his bike.

"Ouch!" He grimaced, tumbling hard onto the road.

He was thinking how out of place a pothole seemed on Minor Street when he heard the sickening sound of a loud crack. He realized his cell phone had gone flying.

"Great!" he said, rubbing his bruised knee through a new ragged hole in his jeans. He limped toward the phone and picked it up. It still worked, but the screen was a shattered mess under the case protector.

"Mom's gonna ground me for sure!" he muttered, carefully shoving the ruins into his pocket. "That's the second phone in four months!"

The bike didn't look much better. The front tire was bent out of shape like a folded donut and the dinged flashlight was beginning to fade into darkness.

"What else can go wrong?" he whimpered.

Just then, he noticed a glimmer of light around the corner on Shadow Lane. He stared at the light, certain it hadn't been there a few minutes ago. He left his bike on the side of the road and slowly approached the woods, limping alongside it. "My Monday night sure isn't going as planned," he muttered.

The light seemed suspended in the darkness until he got closer and noticed it shone from a cluster of thorny bushes. Half-covered by branches was an industrial flashlight.

"Just what I need for my bike," he whispered to himself.

He got onto his hands and knees to crawl into the bushes to get the flashlight. Startled, Zack felt arms wrap around his waist. A squeaky voice yelled, "Gotcha!"

CHAPTER SEVEN

"Ahhh!" Zack screamed, trying to shake off the arms wrapped around his waist to run.

"Ahhh!" the squeaky voice screamed back, releasing Zack. "What... who is this?"

"Who are you, and why the heck did you hide in the bushes and jump me?" Zack demanded as he scrambled to stand on his feet.

He squinted as the flashlight shone in his face.

"Zack? Or Mack?" the squeaky voice asked, shifting the beam like a demented searchlight with each word. Zack thought the voice sounded familiar, but it was hard to concentrate with the blinding light in his face.

Zack shoved the flashlight aside. "Does that really matter right now?"

Zack noticed that there was a second person there when two voices started cracking up. He snatched the flashlight and pointed it a few inches from their faces. Sol and Amanda appeared in the light.

"Very funny, guys!"

"Sorry, Zack," said Amanda, apparently still able to tell him apart from his twin. "We didn't mean to scare you."

"Whatever," said Zack, trying to downplay his freak out.

Amanda smiled as she added, "Although you have to admit, that was a good payback for the straw wrapper in my fries last week.

We're just looking for my dog, Moose, though. He escaped from the yard again."

Sol giggled. "I thought you were him. When you came crawling in here... I thought I had Moose!"

"Hilarious," Zack said, dryly. He would find a way to get back at them another time. "Have you seen Jordan?"

"Not since earlier in class today, before the power went out," Sol said.

"When I got to his house a little while ago, his mom said he left a note that he was headed to your house to do homework," said Zack.

"I don't know why he would say that" Sol said. "I was up the street at Amanda's working on a social studies project, but Jordan wasn't even in our group. I was about to head home when we noticed Moose had gotten out."

Zack frowned. "I don't get it. Jordan told me to meet him at his house after dinner." He wondered why Jordan had lied to his mom. Something felt off. "I'm going to look for him."

"I want to come too," said Amanda, who lived up the road. "Even though it's near my house, I don't usually go into the woods at night."

"Nah, I've got this," Zack said. Although looking out at the inky darkness of the woods, he wasn't sure what was worse, teaming up with his rivals or going out there on his own. He added, "Besides, what about your dog?"

"We'll look for them both," Amanda insisted. Standing and facing the woods, Zack hesitated. Amanda shoved him forward.

Zack blurted, "Okay, I'm going!" After a moment's thought, he stepped back behind her, adding, "Ladies first."

"Don't even think about it," she said. "Lead the way."

Something chittered from the pitch-black woods. Amanda's eyes darted uneasily toward rustling trees half-clad in shedding autumn leaves.

"Hey, what about me?" Sol asked nervously. "I can help, too. I hope nothing's wrong."

"Yeah, me too," Zack said. "Seems really weird."

As they approached the woods, the trees seemed to come to life. Shifting shadows took on creepy shapes, and a slight breeze rattled the leaves. The woods smelled of damp soil. They could barely see their hands in front of their faces unless they shined their flashlight on them. The blackout had plunged the entire area into complete darkness.

Zack looked back toward the town, and he noticed one distant glimmer dissipating behind the trees. It was the big cross towering behind the church steeple, still gleaming in the night, and it suddenly occurred to Zack what was so strange about it.

"Hey guys?" he asked. "How come the light on that cross doesn't go out when all the other lights in this town do? What's up with that?"

Amanda turned and squinted at the far-off light flickering through the trees. "You're right. I hadn't noticed before. I only moved to Tarrytown a couple of months after you did. I don't know why –"

She was interrupted by a nocturnal bird calling in the distance, the sound echoing like a sad cry.

"I'm sorry, guys. I feel like the trees are going to reach out and snatch me away," Sol said, glancing around as though he expected some forest creature to burst from the woods. "I'm not loving this. We could get lost or hurt out here. Let's head back."

"We can't just bail," Amanda hollered. "We've got to complete our mission."

"A mission?" said Sol. "Count me out!"

"Just because it's creepy out here doesn't mean we shouldn't look for Jordan," Amanda said.

"Yeah, okay," Zack said. He wondered why his arch-nemesis wanted to help so much, but he was glad she did. "We're not going anywhere until we find Jordan. And there's a good chance he's somewhere in the woods."

"Why would he be in the woods anyway?" Sol asked.

"Don't you remember his secret tent?" Zack asked, thinking back on the days before they all stopped hanging out together.

"He pitched it in the woods near the lake. Had everything, like he was expecting an alien invasion. We should head there to look for him!"

"Oh yeah, right," Sol said. "I was the last one to hear about it! He invited me to one of his survival meetings last summer, when I was still new in town. Kind of weird if you ask me. I mean, if aliens can travel across space, I don't think hiding in a tent in the woods is going to make a difference."

Zack said, "Makes sense to me."

"I've been there, too," Amanda chimed in. "It looked like he had the entire contents of his house crammed in there. Canned food, bottled water, sleeping bags. He had this mega camouflage high power LED spotlight, a classic gold-plated compass, and old maps for exploring."

"I think he knows his way around the woods," Sol said. An owl screeched and flapped over their heads.

"Now that you mention it, he'll probably be fine. I'm out of here."

Sol took off running down the path he thought headed to the road, but the road was nowhere in sight.

Zack panned the flashlight around Sol then clicked it off.

"Hey! Turn the light back on!" Sol shouted.

Zack shouted back, "You're not going to get far without your own flashlight. Guess you're stuck with us."

"Ow!" Sol cried, his frightened voice echoing in the darkness.

When Zack flipped the flashlight back on, he and Amanda saw Sol struggling to free his arms and legs from some prickly vines. He looked like he was about to cry as he touched a series of cuts and scratches on his face and arms.

Zack hesitated, and then he and Amanda ran toward Sol and helped him up. Sol glared at them.

"Okay, guess I'm not going anywhere in a hurry," he said. "Let's look for Jordan so we can get outta here."

"Yeah," said Zack. "You need to stick with us from here on out. Hang tight, Jordan. We're coming for you. And your mega flashlight!"

CHAPTER EIGHT

Zack panned his dimming flashlight, looking for a path that would lead them further into the woods. As the light shone past a nearby bush speckled with dark berries, Zack glimpsed a metallic disc-shaped object partially concealed in the branches. He slowly approached and shined the light on what looked like a game controller. Curious, he reached through the branches and prodded the object with the flashlight.

"What's that?" Amanda asked, hunched over three feet from the object.

Sol simply hung back, his eyes darting back and forth. He jumped when the distant crackling of leaves rose from the woods.

"I don't know," Zack said.

Zack jumped back as the object slipped from the branches and fell to the ground. He knelt and pointed the light on it. The greenish-black metal shone dully in the beam and displayed several glowing blue recessed buttons.

"Hey guys, what's a game controller doing in the woods?"

"Maybe we should just leave it alone," Sol said, taking a step back. "This is really starting to get weird. What would that be doing out here anyway?"

Zack noticed the flashing central button. Prompted by curiosity, he gingerly touched it with the flashlight and stepped backwards. They stared at this strange discovery for a few seconds.

Zack handed the flashlight to Amanda. Slowly, he reached out and gingerly wrapped his fingers around the controller.

All of a sudden, a loud hum filled the air. Zack, Amanda, and Sol covered their ears as they looked frantically around, Zack still gripping the controller tight in one hand. A vortex of scattered fallen leaves and debris surrounded them. Zack's heart began pounding furiously, and his head pivoted up toward the dark sky. A massive robotic shape of a rocket at least forty feet long loomed directly above them. Blue steam that smelled like wet pennies billowed from its finned exhaust and coiled into the air like fog. Oddly shaped hatches straight out of geometry class covered its dully gleaming metallic surface. Four rubber arms resembling flexible vacuum cleaner hoses loudly bobbed and shimmied out of the hatches on the side of the spaceship, directly above Zack, Amanda, and Sol.

Spectral pinpoints of blue light from the cone-shaped nose illuminated the three of them. An open-mouthed Amanda stood frozen in place while Sol cowered behind her. The humming rhythmically rose and fell in pitch.

Though scared, Zack could not tear his gaze from the mysterious object that swallowed up his clammy hand. His narrow, wet fingers barely locked onto the controller. His parched lips moved, but no sound came out. Somewhere at the back of his mind, he remembered the phone in his pocket. But he did not dare move.

CHAPTER NINE

The wide-eyed trio stared at the hovering rocket. The pulsing blue light cast an unworldly glow into the darkness while the slowly spinning nose cone lit up with electric blue.

"It's aliens!" Sol cried, grabbing Amanda's arm. "They found us! Now they're going to abduct us and stick probes into us!"

"Did you say *aliens?*" Amanda shouted, dropping the flashlight. The two of them bolted into the trees, their fear of the dark replaced by fear of the hovering rocket ship. Zack grabbed the flashlight and shoved the controller into his deep-patched back pant's pocket. He scrambled behind his friends, and the three of them lumbered through the trees to a chorus of crunching leaves and snapping branches.

"It's following us!" Sol squeaked.

Zack glanced over his shoulder at the approaching spacecraft. Hovering above the trees, it seemed the faster they ran, the faster it followed. Something caught Zack's eye from the underside of the rocket. Still running, he panned the flashlight across it.

"What are you doing?" Amanda cried. "Come on, let's go!"

The slinky hoses glimmered and bounced toward them like arms but missed them. Sol looked like he was about to burst into tears.

"Look!" Zack shouted. "There's something on it... words. The... The Skyjumper!"

"What is that supposed to mean?" Sol gasped.

"I – I thought The Skyjumper was the newest, hottest video game on the entire planet," Zack panted. "Funny, Jordan never mentioned that it involved an *actual rocket ship.* Seems like kind of a key detail!"

"We gotta get out of here," Amanda shouted. They were near the edge of the woods, the Skyjumper's lights reflecting onto the shimmering surface of the lake just past the trees.

"Let's head toward the lake," yelled Zack. "We can swim to the other side to Jordan's tent."

"There's just one problem with that plan," Sol shouted above the hum of the rocket. He cupped his hands like a horn around his mouth. "I can't swim!"

"What?" Zack panted, barely avoiding tripping over a root. "Didn't you take swim lessons last year?"

Zack glanced over his shoulder at the rapidly approaching rocket. "Never mind, just run!" he shouted. One of the arms was snaking through the trees toward them. He wildly panned the flashlight and noticed the road to their right.

"Go right!" Zack shouted. "We're not that far from that road! I think that's Shadow Lane. I see a glimmer of light."

They barged through the trees. The path was within reach when the Skyjumper jumped toward them in a blur. As one of the slinky arms arced over their heads above the open path, it emitted a beam that trapped them in swirling blue light.

"I can't move. I'm trapped!" Sol cried, his eyes bulging in terror.

"Me too!" Amanda shouted above the rising hum.

Zack tried to move, but his feet felt like they were planted in the ground.

The air crackled with static electricity and smelled like an approaching thunderstorm. He started to panic, then he spotted a bush nearby. Most of the leaves had shed, revealing several sturdy branches.

"Sol, Amanda, try to grab that bush and pull yourself out!" Zack yelled.

They jerked like marionettes, but none could breach the beam.

"I can't move!" Sol shouted. "It's too strong!"

As they continued to struggle, the slinky hose transformed into a transparent tube that covered the blue beam. The humming grew louder. Suddenly, a strong gust from above knocked Zack, Amanda, and Sol to the ground. One by one, the muffled screaming trio was sucked feet first into the Skyjumper's belly, first Sol, then Amanda, then Zack.

Zack twisted and kicked. "Sol, Amanda!" he cried, but all he could hear were his friends' muffled screams.

CHAPTER TEN

The beam deposited Zack along with some dirt and crushed leaves onto a cold metal floor. Zack flinched when his exposed back felt the cold beneath him. He cracked his eyes open to see a glaring cockpit in his face, humming with massive floating screens and flashing colored controls and instruments. The hatch thudded shut with a resounding clang. Pressing against the cold metal, Zack sat up too fast and reeled from a wave of nausea while spitting up dirt, grass, and roots.

"Whoa!" he said, coughing while taking a few deep breaths until the queasiness passed.

He blinked against the strobing lights and took in a streamlined cockpit worthy of a space shuttle. Something about the air didn't sit right. It felt heavy against his head, as if he were swimming a few feet below the surface of a murky pool.

But he had found a game controller. It couldn't be a space shuttle. So, where did it come from... and why?

He looked behind him and noticed Sol and Amanda lying face down near the closed hatch.

"Sol, Amanda?" he asked, gently shaking them.

Their clothes and shoes were half-shredded, missing shoelaces and exposing their backs. Zack noticed patches of hair on the floor. He gingerly reached for his scalp and felt a clump missing from the back of his head.

"What... ?"

His stomach lurched as the Skyjumper sharply rose. The instruments flashed in response to its movements. The screens jumped to life, displaying scrolling data. A perpetual hum rose and fell in pitch, and Zack felt a strong vibration course through his entire body. In a way, it was almost like looking at a game console.

Gradually, Zack's fear transformed into curiosity. He grabbed onto a nearby wall and pulled himself to his feet. His stomach swam from the sudden motion, so he took it more slowly. Once he got his balance, he walked past the cockpit in the center of the Skyjumper. He peered at the screens but could not understand any of the information displayed. Some of it looked like numbers, but whatever the lettering was, it sure was not English.

A brightly lit tunnel snaked toward another room off the left side of the center of the cockpit. Zack glanced at a still unconscious Sol and Amanda. His curiosity pulled him away from them into low arched circular tunnel. It opened into a room that looked like a computer server room he'd seen pictures of in his dad's office. In the center, slim black towers lit in a dull red glow flashed strange patterns and symbols. Zack smelled a peculiar odor of wood smoke and vinegar.

Noticing a pair of round windows at the back of the room, Zack cautiously approached. They sat flush into the metal wall. He glanced outside and noticed the Skyjumper was hovering above the dark town. Alarmed, he bolted back to the control room and roughly shook Sol and Amanda.

"Wake up, guys!" he shouted. He slapped their faces. "Come on! Wake up!"

Sol and Amanda groggily came to. They sat up and glanced around in shock.

"Whoa, this is..." Sol started to say, then touched his head. "Ouch! My head. What happened to my hair? And what is this place?"

"My new sneakers!" Amanda cried, staring at the tattered remains of her hi-tops. "Mom's gonna have a fit. She just bought them for me last week."

"You're worried about your sneakers?" Sol said, rubbing his head. "We're in an alien spaceship! And look at us! I look like my dad. And Amanda, you look like the red-head doll my sister gave a haircut to." Sol pressed his palms to his forehead. "I thought I'd never say this, but I want to go home."

"I think I can figure out how to run this thing," Zack said, reaching for the controller in his pocket. "Doesn't this setup remind you of a game controller?"

"You're right," Amanda said, helping Sol to his feet. "You think you can use it to get us out of this thing?"

Zack patted his pockets, but the controller wasn't there. His heart raced. He turned his pockets inside out, but he still couldn't find it.

"The controller's gone!"

"Nice one!" Sol said. "Now the aliens are gonna get us for sure." He looked around nervously. "Speaking of aliens," he whispered. "Where are they? Who's running this thing?"

"The controller must have fallen out when we got sucked up here," Zack said, ignoring Sol as he searched the floor around him.

Amanda started pounding at the hatch, but it wouldn't budge. Sol tried to stop her from making noise, but Amanda pushed him aside.

"You think they don't know we're here?" he snapped. Then he glared at Zack. "So now what? It's called a controller for a reason. How are we supposed to get out of here without it?"

CHAPTER ELEVEN

"Look for the controller!" Zack yelled, scouring the floor by the hatch where they were sucked in.

Amanda and Sol reluctantly followed, but the controller was nowhere to be found.

"It's not here," Amanda insisted. Her back showed through her loosely flapping ragged t-shirt. "Everything we had fell out of our pockets. And it did a Pac-Man on our clothes."

"So now what are we gonna do?" Sol complained. "I'm starving!"

"What!" Amanda rolled her eyes as she parted her dry lips. "Is that all you ever think about? The aliens are..."

"Enough!" Zack said. "There aren't any aliens here. I'm telling you, this is like some kind of giant..."

He paused, his mind racing with thoughts. Suddenly, it was all so obvious. Why hadn't he thought of this before? He looked around and gestured toward the cockpit.

"This is a giant game. But instead of playing it, we're in it."

He moved toward the curved area at the center of the cockpit. It seemed to be slightly larger than the other curved areas, so he figured this might be where the main player would stand. He took a good hard look at the screens and instruments. After a few moments, some of the patterns, and even the strobing of the lights, started becoming familiar.

"What are you doing?" Amanda asked.

"I think I just figured this out," Zack said. "Skyjumper, activate voice command!"

"Whoa!" Sol said as the screens and patterns seemed to respond to Zack's voice. "How'd you do that?"

"Well," said Zack, "I figured that technology this advanced would probably have an analog-to-digital converter that could read the sound waves of my human voice and turn them into digital-"

"Can we command it to do anything? Like, take us back to where it found us and pretend none of this ever happened?" asked Amanda.

Zack cleared his throat. "Skyjumper, take us back to the woods where you captured us."

The Skyjumper's engine purred as it began to smoothly glide away. Zack glanced toward the window and noticed the dense shape of the approaching forest. He felt a huge sense of relief.

"Wait!" Amanda said. "Aren't we supposed to be looking for Jordan?"

"Oh yeah," Zack replied. "Hey, I've got an idea! Skyjumper, I command you to turn on your Global Positioning System to find Jordan Hartley right now."

Suddenly, they started spinning counterclockwise.

Zack shouted, "Time for a tight group hug. Don't let go."

They huddled together, trying to keep their balance, but the faster they spun, the colder it got. Zack yelled in a garbled voice, "Stop! Skyjumper, I command you to stop spinning now."

Immediately, the Skyjumper stopped and hovered while their heads were still spinning and their teeth chattering. Then, they fell face first near the hatch and laid there moaning until their heads stopped spinning. Gathering up his strength, Zack said, "Are you guys okay?"

Amanda whispered, "I think so."

Sol muttered, "I threw up in my mouth and swallowed it."

"Ugh!" Zack and Amanda shouted at the same time.

"What do you think that spinning was all about, anyway?" Amanda asked.

"I guess it was a confusing order," Zack said. "Since Jordan doesn't have a tracker or any kind of set location, the Skyjumper didn't know how to locate him."

"Wonder if the Skyjumper could locate some burgers, fries and drinks for us," Sol said. "I'm starving."

At the same time, Zack and Amanda shouted, "No!" But the Skyjumper lurched like it was responding to Sol's request.

Zack scrambled to his feet. "Skyjumper, cancel that command! Continue to our original destination!"

The Skyjumper sped up as it turned back around. "Guess we've got to be careful what we say around here," said Zack, hoping that they were back on track to find Jordan. He looked out the window in the wall opposite the cockpit, but all he could see was darkness sprinkled by stars.

CHAPTER TWELVE

Zack looked back at Amanda and Sol and then at the two curved areas on either side of him in the cockpit. He bit down on his sun-dried lip.

"Maybe you guys should stand beside me?"

Sol looked uneasily at Amanda, but Amanda grinned. "Co-pilots reporting for duty."

They stepped into the cockpit beside Zack. "It's kinda like when we used to game together, isn't it?" said Sol.

"Yeah," said Zack. "Sorry I stopped hanging out after the NBA Hoop Challenge."

"What was the big deal, anyway?" Amanda asked. "You didn't have to act so ashamed to be beaten by a girl."

"I wasn't ashamed to be beaten by a girl, Amanda," said Zack. "I was ashamed to be beaten. Period."

"I guess I didn't have to rub it in your face the way I did," Amanda said. "But you should have been happy to finally have some real competition."

"Wouldn't it be cool if this game were a competition?" asked Sol.

Amanda nodded. "Like, we would command the Skyjumper to race through the forest, dodging trees around us?"

At the words "command" and "trees," the Skyjumper's screen flashed and the spacecraft lurched. Then, they thudded to a stop.

"What happened?" they all yelled, rubbing their patchy heads where they had hit the back of the cockpit.

"Oh no," Zack groaned. "I guess it heard the command for tree. "Cause now we're stuck in one."

CHAPTER THIRTEEN

"Skyjumper, continue to our original destination," Zack commanded. The Skyjumper jerked but remained entangled in the branches.

"Skyjumper, continue to our original destination," he tried again. And again, the Skyjumper just didn't seem to budge. Zack banged his fist on the dashboard.

Sol shouted, "I want out of this thing!"

Amanda walked over to the window and looked out at the branches enveloping them. "Maybe we need to take it step by step. I mean, the Skyjumper's not human, so maybe it needs us to help it get out of this mess."

"What do you mean?" asked Sol.

"Try this," said Amanda. "Skyjumper, shine the light on the tree! Okay, now move six inches to the left."

The Skyjumper inched sideways, releasing one of the branches caught on its edge.

"Sol, you take the window on the other side," Zack said. "I'll see if I can pan the screen to show above and below us."

Little by little, with all three of them describing what they could see of the tree in the darkness and shouting commands, they inched the Skyjumper out of its tree branch snare.

"I think we've got just one more branch snagging us, and then we're out of here," said Zack. "Skyjumper, move slowly down and to the left. That's it... that's it... now stop! Back up. STOP!"

"Yes, we're outta here!" shouted Sol, pumping his fist above his head. "I can't believe we did it. Amazing work, guys."

"Definitely," said Zack. "I think I like having you guys on my team a lot better than playing against you. Ready to get out of here?"

"Wait!" shouted Amanda, still standing at the window. "Could that be... It's Moose!"

CHAPTER FOURTEEN

Zack and Sol crowded over to the window and, sure enough, there was the shadow of a yellow Labrador sniffing the shrubs.

"Moose!" cried Amanda.

"What should we do?" asked Zack. "Do we try to beam him up?"

"Only if you want to end up with a patchy-haired dog," said Sol.

Amanda looked around the cockpit for some clue of what to do.

"Skyjumper," Zack commanded. "Stealth power and sound waves on. Now lower slowly."

They eased closer to the ground. Amanda pressed her face against the glass as she watched her dog glare at the Skyjumper and freeze. A low growl rumbled in his throat, and he flinched, ready to run.

"Skyjumper, stop," said Zack. "Open the hatch."

The door that Zack, Amanda, and Sol had been swallowed up through now gently opened. But the opening was only about the size of a large shoe when the door stopped.

"Moosey!" cried Amanda. She knelt, looking through the partially opened hatch. "Don't be scared, it's just us. Hatch, open please!" But the hatch did not budge at Amanda's command.

Moose took a few steps toward the craft. He stood in the blue light of the Skyjumper, peering up at Amanda through the hatch.

"Hmm, I was hoping we could get this ship low enough to just reach down and grab him," Zack said. "But he's too far away. Should I lower it a little more?"

"No!" said Amanda. "That'll scare him way too much. Or worse, what if you lower it too fast, right where he's standing? No way! You're not moving this thing another inch."

"Well, what are our options, then?" asked Zack.

"Good boy, Moose. Just stay right there," said Amanda. She started scooting herself closer to the edge of the hatch. She carefully stepped one leg down through the hole, but she could not squeeze the rest of her body through the narrow opening.

"Wait, you're not about to jump down, are you?" asked Zack. "There's no way we're leaving you all alone in the woods. At night."

"I wouldn't be alone. I'd be with Moose."

"No, Zack's right," said Sol. "We're better off sticking together."

Zack said, "Sol, you're a quick learner."

Suddenly, the slinky tubes that had sucked the three of them into the spaceship started to lower. Moose howled and ran in circles.

"What's going on? Zack, did you do that?" Amanda asked.

"I think I can get him up here," Zack said. "Skyjumper, locate dog."

"Zack, no!"

Suddenly, *thwonk!,* one of the tubes bounced against the ground. The slinky arms seemed to be flailing uncontrollably.

Amanda raced back and forth between the open hatch and the windowpane. "Moose, watch out!"

"Skyjumper, stop!" cried Zack. The slinky arms settled down and then slowly retracted into the ship. Zack slumped against the wall and wiped a bead of sweat from his forehead.

"Moose?" Amanda called, but outside the hatch was now dark and silent.

"I'm really sorry, Amanda," said Zack. "I was just trying to help. I didn't mean to scare him."

Amanda sighed. "He's a smart dog. He'll find his way home, I'm sure."

"Want to command Skyjumper to take us back?" Zack asked.

"Well, maybe just one more thing first," said Amanda, a lilt of excitement in her voice. "It's called the Skyjumper, right? Well, there must be a reason for that."

Zack laughed and turned to the screen. "I don't know why I didn't think of this earlier, but... do you see any seatbelts?" he asked. "Because we're going to need them."

"Would have been helpful to think of that before this thing tossed us around like popcorn," said Sol.

The three of them found belts tucked in the curved areas of the cockpit and fastened them around their waists. Without wasting time, Zack commanded the Skyjumper to close the hatch and then added, "Everybody, hold on tight."

CHAPTER FIFTEEN

"Skyjumper," said Zack. "I command you to sky jump." The Skyjumper shot up into the air, and Zack felt like his stomach dropped to his feet. Amanda clung to her armrests, while Sol gripped his seat with both arms. But as they leveled out and adjusted to the lightning speed, they gained their footing.

"It's working," Zack said, releasing his seatbelt and approaching the window. He looked outside. At first, he only saw darkness, and then the pale shape of the cross behind the church loomed into view.

"Hey, I see the cross!" he said. Just as before, it was light even while the rest of the town stayed dark.

Amanda joined him and peered outside. "We must be jumping through the sky right over the town," she said.

Relieved, Zack said, "We may just get home after all!"

Zack grinned. He'd always wanted to play the ultimate game, and the Skyjumper was obeying his commands. The only thing he still couldn't figure out was what the Skyjumper actually was, why it was here, and most of all, where it came from.

"Skyjumper!" Zack said. "Return the crew to their posts."

The Skyjumper hovered. The screens and patterns pulsed as though waiting for him to continue.

Zack cast a sideways grin at Sol and Amanda. Amanda saluted.

"Officer Sol reporting for duty," Sol said. "Awaiting your orders, Sir!"

Amanda grinned and did the same. "Captain Amanda to you, boys."

Zack interrupted, "Hold on now. I'm the captain of this mission. But co-captain? That's all yours."

"Oh, all right," said Amanda. "Honorable Co-Captain of Flight 001. Next time, though, I'll take charge."

"I agree. I couldn't have navigated this aircraft without your help," Zack said. He grinned and added,

"And you know what? I've decided you don't need any payback for jumping me in the woods after all. Skyjumper, the master player commands you to quietly drop off Officer Sol in his back yard." The cockpit flashed and pulsed in response as the Skyjumper shifted course.

"Doesn't it need my address?" Sol asked.

"It knew to bring us back where it took us, so I don't think that'll be a problem," said Amanda. "This thing's pretty smart."

Sol and Amanda rushed to the window. "I don't believe it!" Sol said. "It's right above my house! It really did know where to come!"

The Skyjumper shuddered to a stop. A moment later, the hatch clanged open and the blue beam glowed from the opening. Sol stared at it. "I'm supposed to jump or what?"

Zack approached and looked down at the waiting slinky arm. The mild pressure lifted him off the platform.

"It's like some kind of gravity field," he said. "That's how it sucked us up." He turned to Sol. "And that's how we'll get back down."

Sol shook his head and glanced around. "I dunno about that... not sure I trust this thing."

"It's like one of those waterpark slide tunnels," Zack said. "You'll be fine."

Amanda laughed. "Yeah, it looks kind of fun. I'd hold onto your hair, though!"

Sol glared at her. "That's not funny. How am I gonna explain the way I look to my parents?"

Zack and Amanda stared at him.

"Okay, okay," he said. "I'm going."

He approached the now fully opened hatch and looked down. Slowly, he sat at the edge and dangled his legs into the opening. Before he could speak, he was sucked down. Zack and Amanda heard a long squeal, and then silence.

When they both peered into the hatch, Sol was on the ground, disheveled but grinning. He looked up and air-high-fived them.

"See you later!" Zack shouted.

He and Amanda stepped back as the hatch clanged shut. Zack returned to the cockpit and stood in the curve. "Skyjumper, the master player commands you to go to Co-captain Amanda's house."

By now, Zack was used to Skyjumper's responses. It veered away and gathered momentum.

Amanda watched from the window as the Skyjumper slowed and quietly hovered over her yard behind her house. "Hey!" she cried. "There he is! Moose made it back, just like I knew he would."

She ran to the hatch as soon as it opened. She shouted, "You're such a good boy, Moose."

The dog made a low-pitched moan in response. She smiled. "See you at school," she said to Zack. Then, she vanished as the slinky arm sucked her down to her backyard on Shadow Lane where their wild adventure began.

Zack looked down and air-high-fived a grinning Amanda.

"Hey, Skyjumper, the master player commands you to drop Zack off on Mars!" Amanda shouted into the tunnel arm.

Suddenly, the Skyjumper's engines roared. The ship trembled and started to rise. Zack fell to his knees near the window. He caught a glimpse of the cross as the Skyjumper began rising in the sky. He knew he would be lost in space if he didn't react quickly.

"The Master Player commands you to-" Zack gasped, losing his footing as it continued rising, "cancel that order now!"

The Skyjumper responded and slowed to a hover. Zack stood up and turned toward the window to shout at Amanda, but she was already racing toward her front door, Moose wagging at her heels.

Alone in the Skyjumper, Zack felt a combination of excitement and uncertainty. Now he was involved in something from his wildest imagination, the ultimate game. He wondered just how far he could take it. Prodded by curiosity, he returned to the cockpit and took a closer look. Once again, the configuration looked familiar, he just couldn't place why.

As his eyes adjusted to the strobing colors, he noticed what looked like the outline of a human hand in a panel between two screens. In all the excitement, he hadn't noticed it before. He slowly placed his hand over it. He jumped back when it flashed red and slid open to reveal a game controller exactly like the one he'd lost.

"Whoa!" Zack said.

He was tempted to pick it up but wasn't sure if he should. The last time he had touched a controller, it had summoned the Skyjumper. Who knew what this one would do? "Nah, I'll pass," Zack whispered.

That was when Zack thought about me. This was the longest he had gone without hanging out with his brother, and definitely the biggest adventure he had ever had. He realized how much he wanted to go home to the comfort of his parents sleeping on the sofa, to sharing the glow of a video game with his twin.

It had been the strangest night of his life, but whatever Skyjumper was or wherever it came from, he realized it was time to give a final command.

"Skyjumper, the master player commands you to take me to the street in front of my house."

After a few minutes, the Skyjumper slowed down. Zack didn't even need to look at the screens or patterns to know he was home. The hatch opened and the blue beam beckoned. Feeling a sense of relief, he hurried toward it.

He barely felt the descent to the street. The power was still out. He stood in the blue glow and looked up to watch the Skyjumper briefly hover in the air before zooming off into the darkness.

CHAPTER SIXTEEN

While Zack was on the biggest adventure of his life, I'd stayed at home. I had already replaced one set of batteries in my portable lantern when I heard Zack come into the house.

Zack's voice rose from the living room, no doubt giving Mom and Dad some excuse for why he was late. They didn't sound mad at all, though, and a few moments later, Zack came into our room.

I grinned. "So, how was Jordan's?" But when I looked up, I was kind of surprised when I saw his bruised face. Zack always seemed in control, but now, the lantern illuminated an expression on his face I'd never seen before. "What happened to you? You decide to go off-road biking in the dark?"

Zack sat at the edge of the bed and looked at me. He rubbed at a chafed spot on his scalp.

"Yeah, uh, well, I told Mom I fell off my bike." He looked at me for a moment and moved closer. "Mack, if I tell you what happened tonight, you're never gonna believe it!"

"Try me."

I tossed my science book onto the bed and sat up. Zack started talking and didn't stop for almost half an hour. When he finally finished, I stared at him in disbelief. "That's the most incredible thing I've ever heard!" I said. The truth was, I knew a little about what was going on. But I decided to play along. "So, where did the Skyjumper go?"

"I don't know, but I'd be surprised if I ever see it again," said Zack. "Hey, I saw my bike propped outside. How'd it get here?"

Suddenly, Jordan stepped into the door frame. Zack's head swiveled toward him.

"Jordan?!" said Zack.

Jordan grinned. His hair brushed the top of the door-way. "You're welcome," he said. "I brought the bike over a little while ago."

"I'm so glad you're okay," said Zack. "I rode over to your house looking for you. We were thinking you might be out in the woods. I know your tent is well supplied, but it still would have been scary being in such complete darkness during the outage."

Suddenly, the lights came on. The three of us blinked from the unaccustomed brightness.

"Finally!" Zack said. "I've never been so glad to see the lights on. Don't think I'll be going out again when there's a blackout."

"Sounds like you had a big night," Jordan said.

"To say the least," said Zack. "So where were you, anyway? What's up with that note? Why didn't you just text me?"

Jordan smiled. "Let's just say I was in the middle of something," he said mysteriously. "Maybe you guys should come with me."

Zack and I looked at each other and then followed Jordan downstairs. Zack looked more and more curious as Jordan pulled a key out of his pocket and unlocked the door to the basement.

"You have a key to our basement?" Zack asked. But Jordan just grinned and pulled the door open.

Bright light blazed from the basement. Mom and Dad sat at a table poring over laptops half-buried in printouts. The walls behind them were covered with computers, printers, and whiteboards crammed with mathematical equations. I hadn't been down to the basement for a while, so I hadn't seen just what a serious tech lab they had turned it into. And Zack, well, he had been too distracted playing video games to notice.

"What's all this?" he asked, gazing around the basement.

Mom and Dad turned to smile at us. Dad got up from his chair and gestured around the basement.

"Welcome to Skyjumper Central."

While Jordan grinned, Zack and I stared at each other, amazed.

"I don't get it," Zack muttered.

"Why don't you both sit down," Dad said, wheeling a couple of chairs toward us.

We sat and looked at Dad. His eyebrows were raised high, and he wore a giant grin on his face. It was strange to see him excited. "Mom and I got tired of waiting for the government to fix the town's generators," he said. "And Tarrytown's power system is so outdated that buying our own generators would not have been compatible with our setup.

This house was old even when Grandma and Grandpa were living here. When we moved in, we realized just how broken the infrastructure was, and it turns out most of Tarrytown's is the same way. So, we figured out a way to fix the town's generators remotely."

"I don't understand," Zack said.

"I know it's probably hard to take it all in," Dad said, walking to one of the computers mounted on the wall.

He typed in a few commands. A menu appeared on the screen.

"Replay tonight's Skyjumper flight footage."

Zack and I rolled our chairs toward Dad. The screen behind him displayed Zack, Sol, and Amanda on the

Skyjumper and Zack shouting out various commands.

"You mean, you knew about this?" Zack asked, clearly upset. "I went through all of that and you didn't do anything?"

Mom rose and joined Dad by the computer. "You were never in any danger," said Mom. "We had the emergency backup controls so that we could take over operating the aircraft remotely if you were ever in real danger. But we didn't need to, Zack. You, Amanda, and Sol got yourself out of every challenge on your own. Except when we used the controller to keep the hatch from fully opening. We didn't want you to fall out of the spacecraft." We looked blankly at her. Mom came over and gave Zack a hug.

"I'm sorry, Zack. You were all a little roughened up when you were transported into the Skyjumper, so that's something we need to resolve. Probably a weight to height ratio we need to adjust."

Zack nodded thoughtfully and rubbed his head. "Yeah, getting beamed up wasn't the most fun," he said. "I think the whole thing was probably the hardest thing I've ever done. It felt pretty cool to figure most of it out though. And when we were flying over the town and I saw that cross lit up, I knew we were gonna make it home."

I looked at Zack, with checkered patched hair and the bottom of his pants shredded. His shirt looked like an apron with his back exposed. I always knew my brother was smart, but that night, he seemed a little wise, too.

"There's one thing I never did figure out, though," Zack said. "What's the Skyjumper for? All this time I thought it was a game."

Mom and Dad exchanged a glance.

"We wanted you to think it was a game," Mom said. "We figured you'd get into it if it were, and we were right. In fact, we were fully prepared to use the backup controls, but you figured out the correct commands so quickly, we didn't have to, but once. Your video game skills led the way."

"The Skyjumper is a prototype designed to convert the old generators to operate on renewable energy and build new generators for people who don't have adequate infrastructure.

Like us. Then it has to monitor them," Dad continued. "I guess your passion for video games rubbed off on us. We wanted it to operate the way you'd play a game, with a controller. When I proposed the project to my company, they were so impressed that they funded it, and we've been working on it for the past year. Everyone around here got tired of waiting for things to get done, so Mom and I decided to take action."

"That's wild!" Zack said.

"It's genius," I added. "It can convert energy from sources like recycled water, solar power, and even recycled cooking oil."

"Wait, you knew about this?" Zack interrupted. "And you didn't tell me? How come?"

I smiled. "A little. I knew Mom and Dad were working on it while we played our games, but they asked me to keep it a secret. You were always so focused when we played, you never noticed them bringing in new equipment. You know I'm not that great with math or interested in science, so I didn't get too involved with it."

"Wow, bro," Zack said. "I can't believe you kept it a secret from me all this time."

"Are you mad?" I asked.

"I'm not mad," Zack said. "I wished you could have been there in the Skyjumper with me. But... but it was kind of cool doing it on my own, too."

Zack turned to Jordan then. "Wait, how come you knew about it?"

"Your mom asked if I would help out," Jordan said. "To get you to the woods. Hope that's okay."

"And your mom?" Zack asked.

"Yeah, she was in on it, too."

Zack responded, "Did my parents pay you to keep this secret or something? Why didn't anyone tell me the truth?"

"Dad and I thought it would be an exciting surprise for you, sweetie," Mom answered. "We all did. Well, except for Sol and Amanda. They had no idea about any of it. We changed plans to keep this a secret from them. We were fortunate we had calibrated the flight for multiple passengers. But their involvement actually helped us gather important data." She glanced at Dad. "It also showed us how gifted you are when it comes to games and strategies."

"Thanks," said Zack. "That explains a lot. I have one more question, though."

Zack glanced up at the footage of himself in the Skyjumper, still playing behind them. "All of Tarrytown was blacked out. But the cross, it stayed lit. How does it do that?"

"Believe it or not," Dad said, "it's always been that way. Apparently long before we moved here, the cross stayed lit, always."

"Your father's been studying it," Mom added.

"That's right. It inspired me to work on the Skyjumper," he said. "It helped me believe we could bring light back to the island. And we did – with different sources of sustainable energy. But I have to admit, I never figured out the source of light in that cross."

"Know what I think?" said Jordan.

Zack smiled and nodded. "Yeah, I think I do. There is a greater source of power at work here in Tarrytown."

Jordan smiled back.

"Now I have a question for you boys," Dad said. "How would you like to become part of our primary Skyjumper command force?"

"Yes!" Zack and I said together. "Definitely."

"Mom and I will help you to master operating the Skyjumper under our supervision," Dad said. "You might think of it as a real-life video game, but it's a lot more responsibility. When you're older, and you've really shown that you've mastered it, you can become lead pilots."

"Really?" Zack said. "That would be so cool!"

"Awesome!" I said, already getting excited at the chance to pilot the Skyjumper.

Mom and Dad smiled.

"We figured you'd be excited to join the team," Dad said. "But the Skyjumper is only the beginning.

Once it gets certified, we'll build a fleet of Skyjumpers here at the main headquarters south of Tarrytown. They will travel anywhere to convert renewable energy sources, like Mack said."

"Even to other countries?" Zack asked.

"That's our next goal," Mom said. "This technology could help countless people around the world."

"Are you serious!" I said.

"Let's do this!" Zack said.

Mom looked at me, and then at Zack.

"This means studying and helping us as much as possible. After all, we'll be working as a team. It also means you won't have time to play so many video games. Are you both ready to do that?"

Zack and I had no idea of the extent of adventures that lay ahead of us, but we knew one thing. Life in Tarrytown would never be the same. "We're ready."

ABOUT THE SKYJUMPER

The Skyjumper began in my own office, or "cockpit," as Zack would call it, during the fall of 2017. It was there that I began editing my first book for a second publication. But I ended that project within two weeks. I decided it was time to branch out and write a novel. There were two things I initially decided before writing the plot. First, the story had to have a meaningful spiritual experience. Secondly, it had to involve technology. Life has a greater meaning, more than we may ever realize. And technology is exploding faster than we can keep up. I felt like a mad scientist while I was in the "cockpit" creating this technological wonder. Well, not quite – or as Zack would say, "Nah." I felt more like a glad scientist creating a spacecraft that had never been created before. I was the chief engineer. How exciting! And what better place for this spacecraft to present itself than Tarrytown, with its significant problems. The premise and the characters came to life during one eventful night. What makes *The Skyjumper* uniquely suited for this scenario is the characters. They were created just for this adventure. No one else could have gone through the challenges they faced the way they did. As a matter of fact, the characters meshed so well that you will see them again. *The Skyjumper* will become a series of books, so keep your eye out for the next adventure in Zack and Mack's journey.

ABOUT THE AUTHOR

As a child, Glenda Walker enjoyed reading and exploring the rich meanings of words. In 1998, she coauthored her first published short story book for children, *Lovelet Kingdom*. Glenda decided to find other outlets for writing and began writing for her college newspaper. This led her to create a newsletter for a non-profit organization, Grace Abound News, whose mission is to heal the child, heal the community, and heal the world. Glenda's heart is in community activism. She studied Interdisciplinary Studies at Liberty University. She now lives in Connecticut with her husband, Howard. Glenda also enjoys solving Sudoku puzzles and creating reality games, which only adds more meaning and flare to her writing. Glenda was inspired by her faith to write her second book, *The Skyjumper: The Hidden Upside-Down Force. The Skyjumper* is her first middle grade novel.

COMING SOON 2022

THE SKYJUMPER:
Secrets of Alcove Gonosh

by Glenda Walker

SNEAK PEEK BOOK TRAILER

www.theskyjumper.com